TRIAL AND CONSEQUENCES

RANDALL FOX

OAKE FOX PUBLISHING

Cover By Ronald B. Oakes.

Created with Daz Studio and Paint.NET

Paperback ISBN-13: 978-1-971636-05-4

Ebook ISBN-13: 978-1-971636-04-7

❁ Formatted with Vellum

CONTENT AND TRIGGER WARNINGS

This story mentions terrorism, miscarriage, amputation, gun violence, murder, and hate crimes.

This story contains or references profanity and weapons, including the use of weapons, terrorism, speciesism and prejudice, incarceration and imprisonment, homophobia and religious extremism, parental rejection, threatened violence against children, conversion therapy, and suicide.

The story is a science fiction narrative with themes of terrorism, discrimination, justice, and redemption, and it contextualizes these elements within its world-building and plot development.

ARTIFICIAL INTELLIGENCE DISCLAIMER

Grammarly was used to aid with spelling, punctuation, grammar, and word order.

Artificial intelligence was used to aid in generating the Content and Trigger Warning statement text.

Other than as mentioned above, no generative AI tools were used to create the text of this work of fiction.

CHAPTER 1

CHAPTER 1

don't like Earthside time. Mommy and Daddy say I have to spend half the year on Earth for my bones or something. But it isn't like being in space on our ship.

Our house doesn't have my den. Instead, I have a bedroom that is too big. Daddy and Uncle Mark built me a den in the bedroom, so that isn't too bad. It sits on the floor and looks like a wooden box to anyone who isn't a fox. It isn't even half a meter on each side, and has a tiny, round doorway that I can get in and out through. I keep that door facing toward the corner near the hall so it is close to the room where Mommy and Daddy sleep.

Benji and Krissy have their rooms down the hall. Krissy has a den in her room, but Benji decided he wanted a bed in his room instead, so Mommy and Daddy replaced his den with a bed the last time we were Earthside.

The rest of the room was big and empty. Our Earthside house was built for all kinds of creatures, not just foxes. So the doors and ceilings were really tall. But it was close to the trains, which meant we could get everywhere in New Chicago—or almost everywhere.

Our trip from Mars had been bad. Only a few days out, we'd been boarded. Not by pirates, that would have been really scary. We were boarded at thrust, which was scary enough, by creatures from the UC fleet. Before they came through our airlock, Uncle Mark shot me with his darter. That made me sleep really hard. When I woke up, the fleet creatures had taken Uncle Mark away.

And Mommy was really sick. Daddy said she had a miscarriage. I learned that she was supposed to have another kit, a little brother or sister, but something happened and the baby died, or came out early, or something. But that made Mommy sick almost the entire three weeks until flip.

Benji and I both had to be on the bridge during flip, Benji sitting in Uncle Mark's copilot seat watching all of the gauges that Uncle Mark usually watched, and me in the best place on the ship, the sensors chair with the sensors helmet on.

But I had to really focus, because I had to watch out for anything that might hurt us during flip. That meant not only things that might hit the ship, but pirates, too.

When we were in zero-g for the flip, Daddy radioed Earth and Mars to find out about Uncle Mark, but nobody told him anything.

When we got to Luna, where Daddy stored our ship when we had to be Earthside for six months, we learned what happened to Uncle Mark.

Before we boarded the ship that would take us from Luna Port all the way to New Chicago's O'Hare Space Port, Daddy gathered us in the hotel room.

"I received word from Lieutenant Commander Pitt, Mark's Lawyer, today. Mark got a plea deal. He has pleaded guilty to Endangering Space Commerce. He will be serving at least two years at the rehab in Elgin/Dundee. Not too far from our Earthside house."

I looked at Daddy. "Does that mean Uncle Mark is a criminal?"

"Danny, both Uncle Mark and I will have criminal records. But Uncle Mark cannot go into space anymore. They took away his license to do anything on a spaceship. He can't help me. And your uncle won't be able to just be a passenger any more than you can."

A week after we got back to Earth, Daddy had a car take us to see

Uncle Mark, where he was staying. The rehab wasn't anything like the jails I'd seen in my old Pre-cataclysm human videos. It did have a high fence around it. But it wasn't a bunch of buildings with bars holding creatures in cages.

When we got there, a lady cat led us into a room with soft chairs sized for foxes. They even had holes for tails. After a few minutes, Uncle Mark came in. He was wearing a jumpsuit like we all did when on the ship. Except this one didn't have lots of big pockets for holding things. It only had a couple of small pockets. And it was bright yellow, so bright it almost made my eyes hurt.

But that wasn't what was really wrong. Uncle Mark's right arm was gone. At first, I thought he was holding it behind his back for some reason, but then he went to hug Mommy. Uncle Mark never hugs one-armed. Never.

When he bent down to hug me, I could smell too much medicine. I gave him an extra-tight hug.

"Uncle Mark, what happened to your arm?"

"The bad folks shot me, and it… my arm is gone, Danno."

Daddy looked at Uncle Mark. "Mark, why didn't you send word?"

"I didn't want you worrying about me. I've been too worried about you… After I put you all in danger. After I caused Reggie to…"

Mommy looked at Uncle Mark. "That was not your fault."

"The boarding… My arrest… the explosives… how wasn't that my fault?" He was crying. I'd never seen Uncle Mark cry before.

Mommy hugged him again. "Mark, that kit wasn't meant to be; that is all. That wasn't the first kit I've lost. I lost one when Jace was… Before Jace and I were married."

I looked around, all confused. This was grown-up stuff.

Benji walked over. "Come on, Danny. Why don't we sit over here and let Mommy, Daddy, and Uncle Mark talk for a bit, OK?"

I followed him over to the corner where Krissy was on her tablet.

———

Mark leaned back on the bed in his small room at the rehab center. He was tired. An hour of PT, an hour of group therapy, an hour of kitchen duty—cleaning dishes with one arm was trickier than it sounded—and then a forty-five-minute session with the social worker, all before his meeting with Jace, Reggie, and the kits. He needed this half hour of downtime, which was about all new arrivals were allowed during their first two months.

His tablet pinged. So much for downtime.

He sat up, walked over to his small desk, and sat on the hard metal chair. The tablet sat on a stand, making one-pawed operation much easier. He tapped the icon. Lt. Cmdr Uriel Pitt's face popped up in a 2D call from his office at Fleet Legal in New Brussels.

"Commander, what are you calling about?"

"The prosecution in the Mathias case wants to schedule a prep session the day after tomorrow. Raiden Holt and I will be out on the suborbital in the morning and will meet with you for three to four hours in the afternoon."

"How nice, a break in the routine. Spending the afternoon with two lawyers practicing how to answer questions, instead of an extra hour of PT, career counseling, group, and whatever chores they decide a one-armed fox can do around here."

"Mark, you know your calls are monitored. A defeatist attitude is one of the things that can get you held past the end of your minimum."

Mark sighed. "Sorry, it has been a hard week. And I saw the family today. I had a, not really a fight with Jace and Reggie. They kept trying to tell me I wasn't at fault for Reggie's miscarriage. My social worker tells me I'm supposed to take responsibility for the harm my actions caused. And then my brother and sister-in-law go and try to dismiss one of the most tangible bits of harm I caused."

"Did you apologize to your nephew for shooting him? Did you explain why you shot him?"

"It didn't come up."

"It will in two days. We have to prepare for how you are going to answer the question of why you shot two members of your own crew with a darter."

Mark looked at Pitt's image on the screen. "Why is that going to come up at all?"

"We don't know that it will, but the defense might bring it up to discredit you. They are going to do everything they can to make you look bad in the eyes of the jury. The fact that you shot part of your own crew when you almost certainly knew that it was the UC Fleet boarding your ship looks bad, at least it can be made to look bad."

"Ramon would have shot the boarders, or he would have shot the kits to keep them out of the hands of the pirates, I don't know which. My berth was next to his. He talked in his sleep. He'd been one of the first creatures on the Cunningham Family Freighter after it was cleared of the pirates, but before the victims... He saw what they did to the kittens. I knew he had lethal weapons and was ready to use them to keep us safe, but I had no idea what that would mean."

Pitt looked at him, or at least that is what Mark assumed the glance was. "Danny was easier. I didn't want him to see me get arrested... to see me surrender to the Fleet cops. I didn't want him to see me get cuffed and dragged off the ship. I'd have darted Benji and Krissy as well if Jace hadn't knocked the darter out of my paw."

"That is the kind of frank honesty you will need on the stand when testifying against Xandra Mathias. And that is the kind of frank honesty you will need with your therapists in rehab if you want the program to be successful so that you can be released in your two-year minimum."

"Thank you, Uriel."

His tablet chimed. It was time for him to head to his afternoon PT session. "I have to go. I have to do more work on the stump... the residual limb to get it ready for when they can fit me with the cybernetic prosthetic."

"See you in two days, Mark."

Mark tapped the "end call" icon, then turned and walked out of his room and towards the medical building where his PT appointment was.

Louis looked around his tiny apartment. There hadn't been any space available in New Brussels, at least not without paying rent. As a UC citizen, he had his housing guaranteed, but that didn't mean every house and apartment was available. And New Brussels had many rental apartments because many government jobs came with actual salaries.

His last job had come with a stipend, not a salary. But the former UC Fleet Lieutenant Junior Grade hadn't worried about saving his stipend. He hadn't expected to be discharged early. Just a few weeks earlier, he'd been studying the exams that would allow him to move from EOD administration to forensic science, where he'd have more opportunity for advancement. He'd also been preparing to propose to Patrick Bass.

Now, he was married to Pat and honorably discharged, which was better than Pat, who was locked up in the UC Fleet disciplinary brig in New Brussels, awaiting transfer to the main brig on Luna for the first three years of his sentence. But he had to testify against Xandra Mathias first.

Louis looked out across the city of Old Brussels, where he had found an apartment. This apartment wasn't just Pre-cataclysm; it was old. It had been built in the 1920s of the human common era. And it was built for humans, not lobos, or Mexican wolves, as some folks still insisted on calling his species. When he moved around, his ears brushed the ceiling. And he had to duck to move through the doorways. But it was close to where Pat was, at least until he moved to the prison on Luna.

Louis couldn't be near Pat on Luna. Those three years would be as much a punishment for him and for Pat. Their love was new; they'd only been a couple for six months, and it had been a secret for most of that time. But Louis knew that Pat was the man for him. He'd never expected his mate to be a human. But love was… love.

The sun was setting on the gray late November day. It had snowed every day since he'd reached Europe. It was cold here. Even with his thick natural coat, it was too cold. Part of that came from living his last several years on the Sparrow and the Hawk before that. He hadn't been Earthside since the academy, and that was five years before. Being an orphan—being orphaned due to a car crash at 17—can do that to you.

He still remembered that night. He'd been home alone at his home in Albuquerque, still a senior in high school, when the doorbell rang. The police officer had been small. A cat, if he remembered correctly.

"Louis Martinez?" the officer had asked when he answered him in his jeans and t-shirt, tablet dangling from one paw.

"Yes."

"There has been an accident…"

That was it. A jack hare driving his car in manual while plastered hit his parents while they were crossing the street from the restaurant where they had just finished celebrating their 18th wedding anniversary.

He shook his head. He hadn't thought about that day in more than eight years. He'd moved on. An aunt he barely knew moved in to let him finish high school without having to move, then he went to the academy in San José, and from there he posted on the Hawk, then the Sparrow.

Now, he was a former fleet officer. He'd been trained in fleet administration and EOD administration. Almost nobody needed wolves who knew how to babysit EOD lockers for six hours. He needed a job, at least one that would hold him for the five years he'd remain Louis Martinez.

He knew in a bit over five years, he'd have a new identity somewhere neither he nor Pat had ever lived, somewhere that they would be unlikely to run into anyone who knew them. Too many humanists would consider Pat a traitor, so they would have to go into hiding once Pat was rehabilitated. He had no idea where that would be, or what career he might have there.

He settled into the only chair in the apartment that was large enough to hold a fully grown wolf and picked up his tablet. He started flipping through job listings in and around Brussels and New Brussles. If there were any that he could do with his training, he'd apply. But he also needed to know what training he might need for the other in-demand jobs.

There were a few he might be able to do. The government needed many administrative clerks. Paperwork was paperwork, even if nobody had used paper since well before the cataclysm. His fleet train-ing, even if it were focused on tracking confiscated and obsolete explosives, would carry over to many other government functions. There were even a handful of civilian jobs in the fleet he could apply for.

Before he wandered into the bedroom and the too-small bed, he'd sent off a dozen applications.

As he was falling asleep, he looked off in the direction of the fleet's disciplinary brig. "Pat, I love you. Be safe."

CHAPTER 2

CHAPTER 2

kind of liked taking the suborbitals. It was almost like being in space, or at least almost like being on a shuttle. But there were a lot of things I didn't like about them, too.

Early one morning, Mommy and Daddy woke me up, along with Benji and Krissy. It was still dark, and the snow was falling heavily. It was cold on our paws, so we put on our heavy coats, our knit hats, and even our mittens before we walked to the end of our block to catch the tram to the train station.

While we were on the tram, I kept picking snow out of my foot-paws, because it was packed in there and cold. I had snow on my tail, too.

We then took the train to O'Hare space port, but we didn't go to the part where we would if we were going to Luna or one of the space stations. We went to where we would catch the suborbitals.

Our suborbital was out of gate M47. That was a long walk from where the train dropped us. We got to ride on some moving sidewalks.

When we got to the gate, Mommy went to a restaurant only found at O'Hare spaceport to get us breakfast, even though it was still too early and too dark for breakfast. The place was called McDonald's, and they claimed to have once had locations all over the world, but now they were just at O'Hare. Their food had silly names, like Egg McMuffin, for what was egg and ham on bread. It was all made in a food synthesizer, but it was breakfast.

Soon, we all got on the suborbital. This wasn't like getting on a launch. We walked down a square boarding tube, onto the suborbital, which sat on wheels level with the ground, and then to our seats. We had five seats all in one row. Mommy and Daddy sat on one side, where there were two seats. Benji, Krissy, and I all sat on the other. Of course, I got stuck sitting in the middle.

One thing I didn't like about suborbitals was the restraints. They only had lap belts. I wanted proper five-point restraints to feel secure. I liked being hugged into my seat. I even secured the crotch strap, which most folks only secured when they were made to. Because I wasn't properly strapped in with all five points, I spent most of the flight with my tail on my lap, running my paws through it. That helped me not mind that I wasn't properly strapped into the seat.

Once everyone was on the suborbital, it rolled out to the runway, took off, and, once in the air, went up almost like a launch, but not as high. I could see the sky getting lighter out the window next to Benji, who was on his tablet, not even enjoying being by a window. But then it started getting dark as we got closer to space. But we never actually got into space. Then we started down, landing an hour later at what the pilot said was Northwestern Europe Airport.

Then we had to rush out of the airport to the train station next door to catch a train to New Brussels. Even though it was early morning when we left New Chicago, it was almost lunch time when we got to Europe because it was so far around the Earth.

In New Brussels, Mommy and Daddy took us into a big building.

"We are going to support Uncle Mark," Daddy explained. "He is going to be testifying in court against the human who tricked him into putting the explosives on our ship."

Mommy looked at us. "You need to be on your best behavior. That means sitting still, no talking, no squirming. If you need to use the toilet, quietly let me, Daddy, or Benji know, and we'll take you. Benji, you need to behave, too. And you can't be on your tablets while in there. Turn them off before you go in. Off, not quiet."

We all looked at Mommy and Daddy.

"OK, Mommy," I said. I wanted to support Uncle Mark.

Benji and Krissy both nodded.

————

Mark looked across the courtroom as he was led out by the assistant bailiff. Cmdr. Pitt had made sure he was in his suit and even had helped him tie his tie, making him look respectable to the jurors and the folks in the gallery. But that was slightly ruined by the fact that the UCBoRS insisted that he remain restrained while not in the rehabilitation center, so his ankles were manacled, forcing him to take short steps.

As he scanned past the table where Pitt sat with a stag, who had to be Raiden Holt. He saw Jace and Reggie in the second row. In between them sat Benji, Krissy, and Danny. His tail gave a bit of a wag at seeing his family. They were here for him, but that also meant they were here where anyone who was here for Xandra Mathias would also see them.

He then saw the other table. This was only the second time he'd seen Xandra Mathias. But seeing her again made his stomach cold. He remembered her expression as she casually told him that Danny and his human friend might suffer an accident. At the time, he'd missed the hatred. But now… She had the same look on her face as she watched him walk up to the witness stand.

He forced his ears and tail upright. He had to avoid any signs of fear.

He could see that the jury was a mix: canines, felines, rodents, ungulates, equines, and one single human. The canines would recognize if he showed any signs of fear. The others would probably know them too, since canine emotions were considered among the more easily read by other species. The overwhelming scent coming from the heating system probably meant that nobody could smell any stress or fear pheromones, which might be deliberate, keeping jurors from being prejudiced by instinctual responses.

Mark stepped into the witness box.

The bailiff, an older bloodhound, walked up. "Mark Bartlett, do you swear the testimony you are about to give in this proceeding is the truth?"

"I do."

"You may be seated."

The stag stood behind his table. "Could you please state your name for the record?"

"Mark Benjamin Bartlett."

"Mark, how were you employed as of about September 15 this year, Earth Dating?"

"I was the second officer of the freighter Bartlett Family. My duties included serving as co-pilot, navigator, cargomaster, and working with her master to acquire cargos to transport."

"In this last role, did you post a message to the message board 'Dog Walkers Wanted' on Cesar 32 of the current Martian year?"

"Yes, I did."

"What is the nature of the Dog Walkers Wanted message board?"

Mark looked around. "It is a place to exchange cargo on the Martian grey market. The cargo contracts negotiated there are often for goods that are legal to transport, but might not have everything done completely within Mars, Earth, or UC laws."

"Could you provide an example?"

"If someone was selling Martian Whiskey, but had not been able, or willing, to pay the UC transit duties, or the Earth import duties, they might offer it on the Dog Walkers Wanted with forged tax stamps for less than what the same whiskey would cost the shipper from a more legitimate wholesaler with all of the duties paid."

"Did you get responses from this posting?"

"Yes, I got some that led to cargo that Jason, my brother and captain, and I were willing to carry."

"So, you admit that you regularly carried cargo outside of the strict limits of the law."

Mark gave a slight smile. "There are few small cargo carriers that can survive within the strict limits of the law. If there are any, I'd actually be surprised." Inwardly, he worried about that. He was going to have to do exactly that, or Jason was, if he was going to help them with the business side of things. He couldn't go near the gray markets anymore.

"Were you approached by anyone you were uninterested in?"

"I was contacted by a seller, a shipper actually, who made an offer that was a bit too good. XHum000. By the conventions of the message board, XHum000 would be a human with a personal name beginning with 'X,' not that everyone strictly followed those conventions."

"Did you accept this offer from XHum000?"

"No, in fact, I told them I was not interested."

"Did they accept your refusal?"

"No, I finally decided to set a face-to-face meeting to tell them 'no.'"

"Did you meet XHum000?"

"I met a female human in one of the industrial domes at Martian midnight. She strongly implied that she was XHum000."

"Is that woman in this courtroom?"

"She is sitting at the defense table, on the right side."

Holt looked at the judge, a red panda. "Let the record reflect that the witness described the position occupied by the defendant."

"So noted," the judge replied.

"Mr. Bartlett, at that meeting, what happened?

Mark looked at Danny. He hadn't told this part to Danny, or even to Jason or Regina. "The human showed me a video on a tablet. It appeared to be a live feed. It showed my nephews, Danny and Benji, asleep in their hotel room. Then she told me that she knew Danny had a playdate the next day with a human child he'd met a few days prior while we were on Marsport. She stated that an accident could happen to them."

"How did you interpret that?"

"She was threatening to kill my nephew if I refused."

"Thank you. The United Creatures have no further questions at this time."

The defense lawyer, a human naturally, rose. "Mr. Bartlett, do you have a criminal record, prior to any events related to this case, I mean?"

"I have a single juvenile offense in the Martian courts, but per Martian law, that is sealed."

"What about your brother Jason Bartlett, the master of Bartlett Family Freighter?"

Mark looked at Jace. He was under oath. "He has a record on Mars for drug importation."

"Is your juvenile offense related to that?"

Cmdr Pitt stood. "Objection, Martian juvenile records are sealed."

The judge looked at the defense lawyer. "Sustained, please move on."

"Where do you currently reside, Mister Bartlett?"

"Elgin/Dundee, North America."

"Can you be more specific?"

"I am currently a resident of the Elgin/Dundee Rehabilitation Center."

"Were you sent to the rehabilitation center for actions related to this case?"

"Yes, I am there as a consequence of a conviction for Endangering Space Commerce."

"Were you first charged with more serious charges, including terrorism charges, charges that would have resulted in a potential life sentence in a punitive institution rather than a rehabilitative one?"

"Yes."

"Did your agreement to plead guilty to the single charge of Endangering Space Commerce include an agreement to testify against Xandra Mathias?"

"No…"

"So you were given a short stay in rehab because the prosecutors thought you were a cute fox?"

"Objection, my client was still answering the question."

"Sustained. Mister Bartlett, please finish your answer. Mister Clark, please do not talk over the witness."

"No, I agreed to cooperate with the investigation fully." Mark took a breath. He had gone over this potential question with Pitt and Ms. Cruz, the mouse that Holt had sent to Elgin/Dundee in his stead. "At the time I entered into the agreement, I had not seen any images of Ms

Mathias. I later identified multiple images of her from an image array."

"When the UC Fast Frigate Sparrow was following your freighter, were you aware of the pursuit?"

"Yes."

"Did you inform the ship's captain?"

"No…" Mark looked at Jason, whose ears were flat.

"Why didn't you do that?"

"I knew it was a UC fast frigate. I knew that I'd fu… messed up badly. They would only have sent a fast frigate if whatever Mathias had me take aboard was really bad. I didn't want to make those last few days any worse than they had to be."

"You could have stopped the ship, or had your brother stop the ship."

"Two of the three kits are under thirteen. UC law requires that any child of any species be on their home planet at least six months out of the year until they turn thirteen, and then four months until they turn eighteen. If Danny and Krissy did not complete the transit to Luna and then down to Earth on our current schedule, Jason and Regina risked having custody taken away for child neglect."

He looked at his family. "The delay caused by going to zero-g for even a few hours would have made it nearly impossible for them to have made that schedule, even if the ship was capable of thrusting as high as 1g."

The human picked his tablet up and flipped through it.

"When the UC Sparrow caught up with your freighter and prepared to board, you shot two members of the complement with sublethal darts from a civilian dart gun, correct?"

"Yes."

"Why did you take that action?"

"Our maintenance technician, Ramon DeSantos, was a crew member of the UC Nightingale. He was part of the maintenance crew who boarded the Cunningham Family Freighter in the immediate aftermath of it having been violently attacked by pirates. He was a witness to the aftereffects of the atrocities committed against that family of cats."

Mark swallowed. "He has nightmares. He talks in his sleep. I knew about that. He also had a pair of 1mm slug throwers. I believed he would likely react to the boarding alarm as if anyone boarding were pirates who would do grievous harm to the crew, including the three kits. I feared that he would either shoot the members of the UC boarding party, or my niece and my nephews, intending to kill them."

I had to look at an empty spot in the courtroom to say this next part. "I shot him so he would not have a chance to do either."

Then I turned to look Danny in the eyes. "Then I shot my nephew, Danny, because I didn't want him to see me when I turned myself in. I knew that I'd probably be pushed to the deck, cuffed, and dragged off the ship. I feared that would be the last image he had of me. I hoped that he'd be one of those who forgot what happened for a few seconds before they were hit with the dart, and he'd never remember I was the one who shot him."

Mark let his ears drop. "Danny, I'm sorry. I'm so sorry I shot you."

Mr. Clark looked at the judge. "The Defense is finished with this witness."

Holt rose one more time.

"Mr. Bartlett, when did you become aware that Xandra Mathias had put explosives aboard the Bartlett Family Freighter?"

"After my arrest, when I was informed of the nature of my charges."

"Thank you."

The bailiff looked at Mark. "You may step down."

CHAPTER 3

CHAPTER 3

Pat sat in the changing room with his lawyer, Captain Sutton Underwood. The female wolf was one of the highest-ranking members of UC Fleet Legal on the defense side. He should trust her advice and her knowledge of both UC law and the UC Fleet Code of Military Justice. But he wasn't sure he could quite believe her on this.

"Ensign, just put on your uniform."

"I've been dishonorably discharged, or at least demoted to Fleet Recruit/Prisoner."

"No, you haven't. You are not discharged until you have finished rehab, and remain an officer until then. Both the prosecutor and I agree you need to step into court in your full dress uniform, with every decoration you have earned. The jury needs to see you as a decorated fleet officer."

He looked at his uniform with its pitiful one line of decorations. "Not that you get many decorations sitting in engineering watching hydrogen flow into the reactors night after night for two and a half years. Every one of those decorations is either for not getting a blister on my arse for another year, or one everyone on Sparrow got."

"There will be only two creatures who ever served in the fleet in front of the rail in the courtroom today, you and me. None of the jurors will have a clue what any of those decorations mean. They will see that you have them."

"And they will see that the wolf sitting at the prosecution table has four rows of similar decorations."

"They will also see that my uniform has a captain's rocket, and yours has an ensign's gold bar. Even if they don't know decorations, most civilians have at least a basic understanding of officer rank insignia and that it takes time to go up in rank."

She then leaned forward. "If I have to play dirty, I will. If you insist on wearing your prisoner's jumpsuit, I won't let you have a coat. It is snowing out there, and about three below zero. And the wind is blowing. But your uniform comes with a nice coat to wear over your shirt and tie. If you were a wolf, or anyone else with a proper fur coat, maybe the cold and snow."

He sighed. "You… you are not allowed to tease me about being a hairless human. I let Louis get away with that because I love him… and he didn't know I was raised a humanist until… until I nearly killed him and everyone else I knew because…"

"Ensign, you can't break down in court… at least not until it is at the right time. We need you to identify the defendant and lay out, to the best of your knowledge, what she intended to have you do. Then, when the prosecution gets to redirect… if the defense does what we expect, that is when you can get all emotional, got it."

"I'll try."

"Your doctors gave you stuff to take the edge off today, right?"

"But not too much, I have to be sharp."

"OK, now get dressed. I'm tired of looking at a human in his underwear. That is way too much of a hairless, tailless creature to be looking at."

"My husband likes how I look."

"He's weird."

———

Xandra sat at the defense table for the fifth day of her trial. William Clark was not her lawyer, or at least not her original lawyer. Roger Fitzwilliams was sitting somewhere in the same massive jail complex southeast of New Brussels, where she'd spent the weeks since they'd brought her to Earth.

Clark hadn't even been able to argue that it was unfair to try someone who had spent her entire life, actually, a fifth-generation Martian on her father's side, on Earth, where gravity was 2.6 times as strong.

Instead, they had kept all of the Martians on the special acclimation ring of the station for the six-week program to acclimate them to Earth's gravity. Six weeks of physical therapy just to sit in jail before her trial.

Clark was supposed to be the best human defense lawyer on Earth. She thought about hiring a beast as a lawyer to show folks that she wasn't really a humanist, but she couldn't quite trust any of them with her secrets, and lawyers have that annoying habit of insisting that you tell them the truth, so that they can lie for you, or something like that.

But she wasn't sure whether Clark was doing a good job. He'd let the fleet wolf and the UCIS tiger present the evidence about the explosives and that part of the case without hardly challenging any of it. Then he allowed that fox she had suckered, well, bullied, into carrying the explosives into the trap that would get them onto the Sparrow earn sympathy from the jury, and made her look bad. She should have found a better way to force him than to threaten that baby fox, but they needed to move. Her sources in the MBI told her that they were close to finding the explosives.

Now Bass was going to testify. He could do the most damage. If Clark didn't destroy him, make it clear to that jury of mostly beasts that Bass wasn't someone they could trust; she was ruined.

She looked up. The lawyers had finished their daily round of arguments with the judge, so she'd have to stand up so that the jury could come in.

She struggled to her feet. Earth's gravity still made her feel like she weighed thousands of newtons. As the twelve creatures and four alternates filled their box, her legs started shaking. She'd been offered crutches, but she refused to look weak. Instead, she wore dresses to court every day so that nobody would see her shaking the few times she stood in public. She had Clark make sure she was in the courtroom before anyone else, and left after everyone else.

Once the jury was seated, she sat.

"The prosecution calls Ensign Patrick Bass."

He walked in. He was in his full fleet dress uniform. That was unexpected. Clark had assured her that he'd either be dressed like a fleet brig prisoner or maybe in a civilian suit. The UC Fleet was respected. That was part of the reason that Humans First! had targeted Fleet Station.

After he was sworn in, he sat in the witness box.

The deer who was prosecuting stood. "Can you state your name for the record?"

"Ensign Patrick Bass."

"Ensign, what was your most recent posting?"

"I was a gamma shift engineering crew member on the UC Sparrow."

"Why did you join the United Creatures Fleet?"

"I was encouraged by individuals affiliated with my father's church."

"And what church is that?"

"My father is the lead pastor at First Baptist in Abilene, North America."

"That would be The Reverend Franklin Bass, correct?"

"Yes."

"He has preached a number of public sermons on the superiority of humans, has he not?"

"Yes, my father is an outspoken humanist, among other extreme viewpoints."

"But affiliates of that church encouraged you to join the UC Fleet, one of the most diverse institutions in the entire United Creatures, the entire Solar System?"

"They were hoping that I'd become a… They wanted a mole, an agent within the fleet. They succeeded."

"So, even as a cadet and an officer, you continued to work with humanists who were not just philosophically or theologically opposed to equality between humans and other species, but were planning actions to upset the current state of affairs where this equality exists?"

"Yes… I think that is a true statement."

"In that role, were you contacted by someone on Mars to support an operation specifically on the UC Sparrow?"

"I was asked by a woman, a female human, to install equipment and software into the communications systems that would allow me to communicate with her on Mars, even when Sparrow was at thrust."

"Is that woman in this courtroom?"

"Yes, that is her." Bass pointed right at Xandra.

"Can the record report that the witness indicated the defendant Xandra Mathais?"

The judge nodded. "So indicated."

"What else were you asked to do?"

"I was then asked to obtain the ability to monitor communications with the EOD, Explosives Ordnance Disposal, team."

"What about after the ship was dispatched to chase and board the Bartlett Family Freighter?"

"I was then asked to confirm that the explosives removed from the ship were to be retained and transported to Fleet Station. It was at that point that I was told that they were to be detonated on Fleet Station, and I was told to find my way off the station as soon as I arrived, even if it meant going AWOL—absent without leave."

"So you became aware of an act of terrorism that would kill thousands of individuals on Fleet Station, and possibly tens of thousands or more, depending on how the stalk connecting the station ot Fleet Base West Africa fell to Earth. Did you report this to your superiors?"

"No, at that point, I was confused. Part of me still believed in the message of human superiority that I'd been taught as a child. I wanted Humans First!, the group I'd been recruited to join, to succeed. But I also wanted to die in the attack because I had become an unrepentant sinner."

The deer leaned in. "What do you mean?"

"My dad taught that it was a grievous sin for a man to lie with a man, or a human to lie with anything other than another human. I had been lying regularly with a male wolf. My dad led me to believe that until I not only quit doing that, but quit having feelings that made me want to do that, I'd end up in hell, in eternal torment. I was ready to die for my sins. It was that belief that I was… fallen that let me continue."

"What happened?"

"I… I left my tablet unlocked in my boyfriend's cabin. I made it easy for him to find everything. My therapist says that was my subconscious looking for someone to stop me. As soon as I was arrested, I did everything I could to stop them."

"Ensign, your right arm is in a sling. Why is that?"

"I was shot when I was being led to the elevator that would take me from the habitat ring to the hub on Fleet Station. Because I had been put in armor, the shooter hit my shoulder, which has been rebuilt, but it is still healing."

"Thank you. The prosecution has no more questions at this time."

———

Louis looked at his husband sitting there in the courtroom. Pat was proudly wearing his dress uniform, the uniform that he knew Pat had disgraced, but also earned. The part of the young wolf that was still a fleet officer, even a few weeks after his discharge, wasn't sure about that. But he'd talked to Captain Underwood when she'd asked him to bring it to the brig that morning. She'd explained why Pat needed to wear it and how he was still allowed to be seen in uniform.

He'd been proud of how Pat had stood up for himself, publicly declaring their love, even if the only outward sign that they were now wed was the silicone band Pat wore on his left finger. Louis had a matching band on his left handpaw, but his was almost hidden in the fur that was already thickening in response to the cold European winter.

The human lawyer, William Clark, probably another humanist

hired to defend the humanist leader, stood and reviewed the notes he'd been taking on his tablet. "Ensign Bass, you testified that you infiltrated the United Creatures Fleet as a mole for Humans First! Correct?"

Pat looked at him. "Yes, that was my original intention in enlisting."

"So you lied when you were admitted into the academy?"

"No, I earned my way in the same way as any student. I... I might have played down my motivations. I didn't list my family as contacts so they would not know that my father was Franklin Bass or that my oldest brother was William Bass."

"During your time at the academy and serving on the UC Sparrow, you continued to lie to your superior officers, classmates, and fellow officers, correct?"

Pat looked down. Louis knew that if he were a canine, his ears would have dropped. "Yes."

"You lied to your boyfriend?"

"I... I lied to him about why I wanted to get to know him in the first place. But not about loving him. Never about that."

Louis had to fight to keep his tail from wagging. He didn't want the handful of humans in the gallery to know that he was Pat's husband. Courthouse security should have kept weapons out, but that didn't mean anything. And if he had to defend himself and was forced to injure or kill a human, the consequences could still be bad, not only the legal consequences, but the psychological ones.

Clark pointed his fat, hairless finger at Pat. "You are very good at lying, aren't you?"

Captain Underwood shot to her feet. "Objection! Argumentative."

The judge, a red panda, looked at Clark. "Sustained."

Clark smiled one of those odd human smiles that was charming on Pat, but disconcerting on this human. "Let me rephrase. Ensign, you spent years deceiving fleet officers, including several of the officers on the Sparrow who worked in law enforcement capacities, for years, correct?"

Pat looked down and replied softly, "Yes."

"Why should the jury believe you now?"

"Because I no longer wish to hide who I am. I no longer wish to hide what I was, what I was part of. What I came close to being part of."

Clark looked at his tablet. "Before you reached the plea agreement that will let you serve a mere five years, only three in punitive custody, you were facing charges of treason, correct?"

The stag prosecutor, Holt, shot to his feet. "Objection! The witness' plea agreement has already been established."

The judge looked back and forth between the lawyers. "This goes to the witness' credibility; I will allow it."

"I might have been charged with treason under the UCFCoMJ, yes."

"Isn't the penalty for treason under the United Creatures Fleet Code of Military Justice an automatic and mandatory sentence of death?"

"Yes."

"So, by agreeing to testify against Ms. Mathias, you have escaped from a mandatory sentence of death to being released from prison after only five years. Is that why you are lying about Ms. Mathias?"

"No, I am doing this because it is the right thing. I am doing it because I need to make amends for being wrong about 24 years of false beliefs about where humans fit in the universe, about who I am, and everything else."

"So, your change of heart about... non-human sentient creatures led you to testify against Ms. Mathias. Did you ever actually meet her? Face to face?"

"Yes. Right before I was posted to the Sparrow, I was on Mars and given a 48-hour leave."

Louis hadn't heard this story before. He leaned forward.

Pat leaned back, looking up towards the ceiling for a moment. "Several of the newly commissioned officers were invited to a reception at the Martian Museum of Art and History. Archeologists had just recovered the Viking One lander, and it was about to be unveiled in the early missions gallery."

He shifted forward. "During the reception, I was approached by an older human woman who was on the museum board. We carried on small talk for several minutes. But as we were leaving, she brushed my watch with her minitablet comm. My watch vibrated, and I noticed that it was now loaded with the unlock code for one of the museum's courtesy lockers."

Pat turned to look at the jury, then over at Holt and Underwood. "Before leaving the museum to return to my temporary berth, I retrieved the contents of that locker. It was various pieces of comms equipment and the instructions on how to install them into the Sparrow."

Pat then turned to look at Matthaias. "That woman was Xandra Matthias. And some of what we talked about was our, at the time, shared humanist beliefs."

CHAPTER 4

CHAPTER 4

Pedro Ballard slithered around the day room of the New Brussels detention center. He'd been locked in there for a week for a simple misunderstanding. He'd been trying to explain to the client, a young female rabbit, that he couldn't simply clear her clogged toilet. The plumbing in her flat, one of the Old Brussels flats dating back to the 19th or 20th century of the old human common era, had to be torn out and replaced.

This was a common problem. The plumbing modifications connecting the old sewer systems to the organic matter synthesizer systems were often poorly executed, and the old iron piping suffered as a result. Plumbing that old was subject to failure anyway.

But she'd started yelling at him, claiming that he wanted more money. He wouldn't get a Euro for that work. He was a snake plumber —hardly more than a plumber's snake. His job was to dive into drains and use his tiny plumbing prosthetics to clear clogs. The Earth-Europe housing bureau would take on the work that needed to be done and contract an actual plumbing contractor.

But she kept yelling, and he got frustrated and his tail started rattling. She claimed that he was threatening her.

Now, he was under arrest, charged with assault with a deadly weapon. It wasn't his fault that he was venomous. He was born that way.

His lawyer was sure he'd get off once he got to court, but that might be in a few weeks. And the judge decided to keep him locked up, so he was stuck in detention.

At least detention wasn't too bad. He had more meals than he could eat. He had access to the feeds. And he wasn't spending his days diving into folks' toilets and sinks. Then again, he could have had the same if he'd just stayed unemployed and bored.

He slithered over to the center's common feed tablets and started looking through the available news. As he flipped through using his prosthetics, he noticed the top headline. "Xandra Mathias convicted on all charges."

He looked further down the article, noting details like "Sentencing would be in four to six weeks," and "faces up to forty years in punitive custody."

His tail started rattling again. His brother, sister-in-law, and one of his cousins were all part of the Fleet Station maintenance crew. Orbital stations with their spinning habitat rings were almost as bad as cities with intact human buildings for drainage problems. And snakes were in demand for their ability and willingness to climb into drains and fix things.

That human had planned to murder thousands of creatures, including three members of Pedro's family.

He then saw her, Xandra Mathias, walking across the common area towards her room. She didn't seem phased at all by the fact that she'd been convicted of multiple crimes related to terrorism. She looked like she was more bothered by the fact that she had to use crutches to walk in terrestrial gravity than the fact that she'd probably spend the rest of her life in a punitive institution.

He wasn't sure what overcame him. He slithered after her, keeping to the shadows.

He slid out of his prosthetics, which made it easier to climb the wall.

He climbed into her cell, hiding in the shadows. She was lying on her bunk, not sleeping, just staring at the ceiling. She was mumbling—not mumbling, talking to someone. She might have a communication device hidden in her body.

He slid onto her bunk. Almost without thinking, he opened his jaws wide. Pit vipers don't have the same kind of hinged jaws that some other snakes have, but he could still open them wide enough. He extended his fangs, and then he bit her. Right in the neck, into the jugular vein. He let his venom flow into her.

He then pulled out and slithered out of her cell and over to the guard post.

He looked at the guard, a large ox. "Guard, something has happened to Xandra Mathias. She has suffered a snake bite to the neck. You should probably call the police and have them arrest me for premeditated murder."

Louis looked across the table.

Pat looked smaller back in his green prisoner jumpsuit. Dark circles had formed under his eyes. His fur—no hair, humans had hair—was disheveled. Pat was letting it grow out, and it was no longer the neat, consistent fifteen millimeters he'd maintained for the entire time Louis had known him.

Louis was sure that some of those hairs were grey as well, which was considered uncommon for someone who was only 24 years old.

"Pat, I can move to Luna to be closer to you." He reached his paw to put it on his husband's, feeling the soft silicon ring under his sensitive pads.

"No, even if you were on Luna, you still would only be able to see me on video calls. It's the punitive brig. No visits, and especially no congenial visits. I'll have to satisfy myself like I did for the ten years before I met you."

Louis laughed. "I didn't know you were a virgin before…"

"Dr. Dawson says we need to deal with the potential lack of consent over that first night."

"We were both pretty wasted. I don't even know who first…"

"I think I asked you. Louis, I've wanted to fuck a canine since I was about thirteen and first realized that I wanted to fuck anything."

"Ensign, you are still part of the fleet…"

Pat laughed. "Sorry, I know I should use fleet language. But what are they going to do, put me in the brig?"

Pat then shifted to put his hand on top of Louis' paw. "I was ashamed and scared. I had a folder of pictures on my tablet. But I had to hide it. I had to download the best security and encryption software, not the same ones Dad used for some of the stuff I've told the UCIS folks about."

He looked at Louis. "You might have had some of the same pictures. They weren't even hardcore stuff. Just naked pics of wolves, dogs, and a few foxes. The stuff you might find in *Foxy Canine Boys*, no, it was actually bootlegs from FCB."

Louis laughed. *Foxy Canine Boys* was an online publication that was absolutely targeted to gay teenage canines, and some others who liked young, but legally consenting, male canines. He'd had a subscription himself when he was 14. His parents actually got it for him, figuring it would be better than what he might find if he went searching on his own."

Pat looked Louis in the eyes. "You have to understand my father, Louis. If he'd found pictures of naked human women on my tablet or printed out and hidden them in my room, he might have hit me. He'd have hit my behind with a leather—genuine leather, not synth leather —belt until it bled."

He paused, swallowed, then continued. "If he'd found pictures of naked human men… There are camps on Earth. They aren't legal, but Dad knows where they are. They pretend to be regular Christian summer camps. But they really are there to cure kids of sinful urges. One of my school friends went to one of those, then took her life the following fall."

He looked back at Louis, tears in his eyes. "Dad owned an antique 9mm handgun. A Glock, Pre-Cataclysm. If he'd found my copy of *Foxy*

Canine Boys, he'd have taken me out into the woods outside Abilene and put a bullet in my brain, and then left my body in the woods for the non-sentient scavengers. He wouldn't have been sad to have killed his youngest son. I think he'd have even preached a sermon about it."

Louis looked at his husband. "Your father still wants you dead, doesn't he?"

"Yes, he's not the only one. Xandra Mathias might be dead, her organization in shambles, and her plans falling apart. But there are still thousands of humanists among the millions of humans spread across the solar system. They might be 1% of the human population who make up 1% of the entire population, but that is enough for me to be in danger."

"But you… We can't go into hiding until you are released?"

"I'll be one of two humans in the penal brig. The other one has been there for 2 years of her 10-year sentence. I can't hide who I am in there. In five years… then we can try to make a new start. UCIS Witsec will keep us safe then, and they will keep us safe before."

Louis laughed. "Right now, they are telling me to live my life, and maybe play down who my absent husband is."

Pat leaned over, or as far as he could with his left wrist chained to the table and his right in a sling, and kissed Louis on the muzzle, before giving him a quick lick on the nose. "Louis, stay here in Brussels, or go home to Albuquerque. Then, when I step down to rehab, come to wherever I am. Then we'll go into hiding together and really start our life. Until then, we'll talk as often as they let me, and know I miss you and I love you."

———

Chief Tobias Shafer slipped into the cold water of the Senne. This was not his normal duty. Leading a party of other otters, a mix of Fleet and UCIS troops, down the river towards the camp was different than leading a boarding party across a docking tube. But as the most senior otter in the joint task force handling the trove of revelations from Human First! raids, he was put in charge of this part of the operation.

He swam downstream at the lead of the team of two dozen otters.

Most were, like him, European river otters. But there were two sea otters, and Isaac Buck, one of the UCIS agents, a giant otter originally from South America, was their communications and equipment specialist.

UCIS had been monitoring the farm northeast of Brussels, where the gorillas lived and worked, since the records recovered from Xandra Mathias' computers had indicated a connection between the European Great Ape Liberation Network and Humans First!

Intelligence indicated that EGAL had planned an attack on the UC Parliament after Humans First! took out Fleet Station. With that first attack thwarted, the second was delayed. The hidden communications equipment found on Xandra Mathias, along with other signs, suggested that EGAL was preparing to act, so it was time for the task force to move.

Chief Shafer checked his position using the fleet's satellites and confirmed it using a few landmarks. Then he nodded back to Agent Buck.

"River Team in position," Buck signaled, which was relayed through the team's earpieces.

"Air Team in position."

"Land Team Alpha in position."

"Land Team Beta in position."

"Land Team Gamma in position."

Shafer raised his right paw and gave a single circle clockwise. He then checked his rifle, a 2mm semi-auto. It was set for 3-round bursts, and the clip had 30 rounds. He had two spare clips. He also had a darter loaded with a double clip, sublethal and lethal, selectable with a flip of his thumb. He slipped on his night-vision goggles. His natural night vision was better than some mammals, but not good enough.

A quick glance back confirmed that his team was all ready, their rifles checked, and night-vision goggles in place.

They waited on the edge of the river, less than two meters of damp, snow-covered ground between them and the barn where the gorillas— gorilla guerrillas, he thought with an internal laugh—waited planning their attack on parliament.

"Execute, execute, execute."

His team emerged from the river. They crossed the two meters on all fours, then rose to their short hind feet to close the distance to the barn. A flash-bang went off on the far side—the signal from the detonator reaching the processors in their night-vision goggles to suppress the flash, protecting them from the sight briefly, but not the sound.

Shafer lifted his right paw, then pointed it towards the small opening in the back of the barn, before running through it.

The barn was already in chaos. More than fifty assorted large primates, gorillas, chimps, humans, and others he couldn't identify were in there. Most of them had picked up either guns or darters and were firing at the fleeters and UCIS agents.

Shafer dropped and fired at one of the closest targets, a large gorilla, who was turning towards the party of otters entering. A single burst from his rifle, and blood blossomed from the gorilla's chest. 2mm might not have a lot of stopping power, but this time, they were enough. The gorilla dropped.

He shifted to the right, shooting the chimpanzee who had just fired a dart towards him. The dart bounced off his helmet at the same time the chimp's shoulder exploded into a mass of flesh.

The firefight continued for an eternity, measured in about thirty seconds.

"Hold Fire. Hold Fire. Hold Fire."

Shafer took his trigger claw off his nearly empty rifle and stood. The barn was a mess.

He turned to his company to assess the situation. Two of them were wounded, including Buck, who had taken a dart wound to his arm. One of the fleet medics was already administering the anti-toxin that should counter the common poisons used in lethal darts.

UCIS Special Agent Joshua Bender, the head of the task force, strode in. The tiger was wearing armor, but his helmet was unbuckled. He had sat in the command vehicle the entire time.

Agent Palmer, a bison who had been in command of Ground Team Alpha, walked over to him. "Sir, we have neutralized the EGAL forces on site. Limited casualties on our side. All suspects down."

CHAPTER 5

CHAPTER 5

Mark lay on the bench, working the band with his stub, his residual limb, as the PT kept insisting he think of it. It was getting easier to move those four millimeters left of his right arm, the arm he used to write with. The arm he used to hold a fork with, used to control the throttle and front brake on his bike, used to control the stick on… no, he couldn't think about that, even if he had a working right arm; spacecraft were lost to him.

"Good Mark. Give me another five, and then you can take a break. Another week, and we can look at taking the scans for your temporary." Oklee Morrow, the babboon PT at the rehab, looked happy, but Mark could never really tell. His face was both too expressive and not expressive enough. Primates always confused him, and the cold he'd picked up on the UCBoRS transport back from New Brussles, which he hadn't fully shaken even after four weeks, made things worse. Four weeks of stuffy noses had to be worth at least twenty points towards his release all on its own.

"The scans will only be for a temporary?" Mark asked.

"It's not because of your status as a resident of rehab. Most creatures don't get a permanent prosthetic at first. The temporary will help you adjust to using one, and will help us change the programming to how you use it.

Mark finished the last of this last set with the band and sat up, something he could finally do without having to use his left paw any more than he used to need.

"So for a few weeks, I'll have one of those obvious carbon fiber arms."

"No, for a few months, maybe a year, you'll have a succession of 3D printed arms. All prosthetics are carbon fiber. If you see someone with one that has the carbon fiber visible, that means that they haven't put the fur sleeve over it for some reason."

Mark looked at the baboon. "Will I be able to ride my bike? I have a vintage Honda 1850 EBike—Pre-Cataclysm, one of the first true all-electric bikes. It was a child's model, obviously. But I've done some work on it, replaced the batteries with a microfusion plant, and updated the motor to increase torque. I had to have someone else replace the shaft with a titanium one that could handle it."

Morrow looked at him. "And that thing isn't what took off your arm? You haven't smashed your skull open with it yet?"

Mark sighed. He should know better than to talk to a medico about his bike.

"I'm kidding you. I have a Kawasaki, a 348 model 9254—pure fusion direct drive. Sweet ride."

"I've rented some 9254s, the Martian variants. I rode one through the tunnels… heck, I was on one the night that I took the wrong turn that led me here, not only into this rehab center, but onto your bed with one arm. Those events are related, so…"

"You lost your arm when someone shot you with ammunition larger than most bones in a fox's body, or at least about the same size, but with enough energy to do a hell of a lot of damage to a large-sized soft primate."

Mark looked at him. "Large-sized soft primates, how many of those are there?"

"I only know of one, humans. Gorillas and other large primates have thicker hides. 7.62 millimeter ammunition is ancient, and was designed to take out one thing, humans."

"It dates to the Sentience Wars?"

"It dates to when humans were killing each other in their own wars."

"And that is what I was shot with. No wonder my arm didn't survive."

"If you hadn't been in good armor, you would have been a smear on the ground, or it would have punched a tiny hole through you, and you wouldn't have been injured much. It would depend on exactly how it hit you."

"So the armor saved my life."

"And made sure that your arm was unsalvageable. I've seen the medical reports as part of the treatment I needed to provide you. At the speed the bullet drove your arm into that armor, it was like a concrete wall."

"We need to get to work, more balance exercises. Onto the BOSU ball."

"No pulling my tail today."

"I'm not promising anything."

———

Pablo looked around the group therapy circle. This was his first group therapy session at the Elgin/Dundee Rehabilitation facility. He had no idea what to expect.

He hadn't actually been expected to be sent back to North America. He'd been raised for his first thirteen years in North America, in Elgin/Dundee, even. His father's family still lived in the area. But after his parents' divorce, his mother had moved to Europe, eventually settling in Antwerp.

She'd died in the reptile plague of 352, when either a deliberate or accidental—depending on who you asked—change to the programming of the food synthesizers caused them to produce a virus that was fatal to snakes, particularly pit vipers. This mainly impacted parts of Europe over a few weeks. Pablo had been back in North America, visiting his father, fighting with his father, more accurately, at the time, so he wasn't impacted. He moved back to Europe and hadn't been in North America since.

But with cousins, the closest relatives not living on Fleet Station, being in the area, this was where he was to serve his six years of "reflection and rehabilitation" for murdering Xandra Mathias. He was still suffering from suborbital lag. He woke up at his usual time of 0630, but that was 2330 the previous night, local time. He lay awake in his room, unable to sleep until breakfast at 0700, when his body thought it was already 1400, well into the afternoon. Now it was 0830, and he was ready for the day to end, but he still had most of it to look forward to, starting with this circle of eight creatures.

The leader, a rabbit named Dr. Callan Mills, the only creature not in the bright yellow jumpsuit—or, in Pablo's case, a bright yellow stocking that made slithering hard—looked around the circle. "We have a new participant in the group starting today. Pablo, would you like to introduce yourself?"

Pablo had been told that open participation, admitting his crime, and expressing remorse would all help him earn the points that would help when it came time to assess if he could get out at the end of his six-year minimum sentence. "Hello, I am Pablo. I am in here because..." He hesitated. He was supposed to show remorse. But he wasn't ready yet. "...I executed Xandra Mathias by pumping her full of my natural venom."

His tongue felt the scab at the top of his mouth from the surgery where his venom glands and fangs had been removed, the other consequence of his conviction, his pleading guilty to first-degree murder. His lawyer had tried to get him to plead to second-degree, but he argued that he had planned to kill Xandra when he went into her cell, so that was the crime he'd finally plead guilty to.

The ears on the red fox across the circle from him went down when he said Xandra Mathias' name. He wasn't sure what that reaction was about. Most creatures knew who she was, but this wasn't the reaction of someone who hated her in the abstract, like he had. This fox knew her.

He half-heartedly listened as the others in the circle went around introducing themselves. Their crimes were quite varied: drunk driving, bank fraud, child endangerment, possession of something the deer wouldn't detail. Then it came to the fox.

"I'm Mark. I'm here because I agreed to bring explosives aboard my family's freighter. Endangering Space Commerce is the crime. I worked with Xandra Mathias, unwillingly, I was one of her victims, and one of her accomplices."

Dr. Mills stopped the next creature from introducing herself. "Mark, how does what Pablo did make you feel?"

The fox looked at the snake. "I… I don't know. I'm glad she's dead in a way. But I don't think he was right to kill her. That wasn't his right. Maybe the UC had that right, maybe they didn't. But he didn't."

"Are you mad at him?"

"No, but… I don't know. She wanted to hurt, no, kill my nephew. She wanted to kill me and thousands for some reason I don't understand. But I don't know if what Pablo did was any better."

"Pablo, how does it feel to know that someone who had been hurt directly by Mathias' actions is right here, and that you will have to face him every day for the next few years?"

Pablo looked at the fox. "I… I guess he'll become one of the reminders that I can't let anger get the best of me."

"Good, that is a start. Let's continue the introductions, and then we can move on with other discussions."

———

Pat walked into the gym. His schedule required three hours of gym time every morning and two hours every afternoon: treadmill, weights, calisthenics, the whole deal. He hadn't had anything like this kind of physical workout since the four weeks of basic training that preceded his three years at the academy. Now this was going to be five hours of his day, every day, for the next three years.

The guard at the door to the gym, a North American badger FFC in duty uniform, saluted, which Pat returned. "Bass, you are assigned to treadmill 17. You need to complete 15 kilometers, no more than 60 minutes, or you will get a demerit. Then come back here for your next task."

He walked over to the treadmill and climbed on it. At least they had given him slip-on shoes like he wore on Sparrow, not the sandals he'd worn in the brig on Earth. He clipped the safety clip to his jumpsuit—the same kind of green jumpsuit he'd been wearing since his arrest on Sparrow, except for the printed ensign's bars, a reminder that even here, he was an officer, almost more of a humiliation than a comfort. He hit start, noting that the program was preset for 4.166 m/s, the pace that would produce his required time over the hour. He started walking at a fairly easy pace. This wasn't going to be hard; he was in good shape, even if his job on Sparrow had been sitting for eight hours.

"First day?"

He turned to see a bear, a hulking brown bear, on the treadmill next to him. "Yes."

"Callen Mills, doing fifteen in punitive for shredding half the bridge crew of the Jediah Crawford after a bad reaction to a dart. Charging the bridge over a denied promotion probably would have landed me here for a few years to begin with."

"Pat Bass… I can't remember what they finally ended…"

"Everyone knows why you are here. Don't worry about me. I'm one of the ones who thinks you are a hero for waking up and standing up."

"So, not everyone…"

"Pat, opinion in here is divided. It's probably 80/20. More are with me that you are a hero. But some of the hard cases still see you as a traitor to the fleet who should have had a needle stuck in his arm."

"So I need to watch out here in the gym or any other time I'm around others?"

"Nah, most of the hardcases who want you dead don't want to die."

"What are you… Oh, yeah. Treason, loss of code book, murder by an inmate in a penal brig, misbehavior before the enemy, and a couple of others that are even more obscure."

"Yup, if they kill you, they are putting a needle in their own arm.

And they won't even get a real court-martial, just a quick review by the panel, then off to the long sleep."

Pat thought about the news he'd heard just before he was put on the transport to Luna, how a snake had killed Xandra Mathias. He was going to get out, but if someone killed him, at least here in the fleet penal brig, they would be subject to something almost akin to summary execution. As bright and clean as the fleet looked on the surface, it had a dark underbelly, and he was now living in it.

Callen looked at him. "Don't worry, you'll get through this. You're here for what, three years?"

"Yeah."

"I'm on my fifth. Three is easy. Just follow orders and don't give anyone grief. Most folks here don't want trouble. Trouble means demerits, and demerits means..."

"Loss of privileges and increased corrective measures. But they didn't even tell me what the latter means when I got here."

"They have you doing 15 klicks this morning?"

"That is what the badger said."

"Get a few demerits, and it will be 30 or 45, still within the same hour. And they will start programming in the hills. You remember those runs in basic, the hills on the east side of the academy?"

"Oh, yes. Where I grew up was fairly flat. Those hills killed me for the first few days."

"That treadmill you are on can go about twice as steep. And don't think that the 1/6 gravity will help; the system accounts for that."

Pat looked around the gym. Other creatures were working on weight machines. A group was in a side room doing calisthenics.

"So what all does the program in here really consist of?"

"Everything you probably hated about basic training, and then some. Part of this is to keep you from getting too weak in lunar gravity. Once a week, you get to spend two hours in the spin and puke, too."

"Oh, God..." Part of Pat winced at the blasphemy, the tiny part that still believed an iota of what he'd been raised to believe. "...I've never had to spend time in a centrifugal gravity correction chamber. I was never Marsside or Lunaside long enough. I spent most of my time in the fleet on Sparrow. I've spent more time at 1.2g than at 1g the last two years."

Callen laughed. "That is just the exercise portion of the day. Then there is the work. Maybe you'll be lucky and get something easy, like the library or medical. What was your role?"

"Engineering, reactor monitoring mostly."

"Crapshoot. Like me, coming from tech research. Maybe I'll see you in the kitchens. A lot of folks work down there. And they don't care if you have a bar on your collar or not. The guards will salute you, then hand you a dish towel."

Pat sighed. "It's weird. On Sparrow, none of the enlisted ever bothered saluting anyone other than their COs. Here, the guards are saluting me like I'm an admiral or something. Even the enlisted prisoners, who I think are all now fleet recruits…"

"FTCs, you can't be busted back to recruit."

"Anyway, they salute me too."

"It's all part of the culture of discipline. If you see any officer of higher rank—and that is anyone who isn't a prisoner—you had better salute unless you want a demerit."

Callen's treadmill beeped and slowed. "I have to go show how strong a bear is, even when he's pushing forty. Talk to you tomorrow, unless we end up standing next to each other at a wash sink later."

CHAPTER 6

CHAPTER 6

Mommy and Daddy hadn't taken us to see Uncle Mark since we'd seen him in court. But finally, just before the New Year, Daddy hired a car, and we went out to where he was. The nice cat showed us into the same room.

When Uncle Mark came in, he looked better than he had before. His fur was combed better, and it looked shinier, more like my fur. And he had a right arm!

His right arm wasn't a fox's arm. It was made of many colors, and even from when he walked in, I could see that it had the same funny stripes as the parts that came out of the 3D printers on the ship and at home that we used to make things.

I ran up to him, my tail wagging harder than it had in a long time. "Uncle Mark. I missed you."

He bent down and hugged me with both arms. His printed arm felt funny where it wrapped around me, and he squeezed me a bit hard with it."

"Is that too hard, Danny? I'm getting used to the new arm. Just got it yesterday."

"It's a bit hard," I lied a bit. Uncle Mark was pinching my side with his new elbow.

He let me go. Then he sat on the floor and tapped it with his left hand.

I sat, crossing my legs and laying my tail across them.

"Danno, I am so sorry I shot you with the dart."

"Uncle Mark, I don't really remember you shooting me." That was a lie, too. I remember him pointing the darter at me, the sting in my chest, and getting all sleepy.

He sniffed. Uncle Mark looked like he had a cold, but his eyes told me he could smell my lie. Why could grown-ups always smell a lie, even when that lie was supposed to make them feel better?

"Danno, I… I didn't want you to see me get arrested. When the fleet arrests someone, they aren't nice about it. They treat everyone like they might hurt them, like they are a pirate."

"I… I… You didn't want to scare me more than you scared me."

"I didn't want your last memory of me to be seeing me taken away like that."

"Uncle Mark, if you hadn't come back, I'd have remembered you shooting me and not knowing why." I was starting to cry. I tried to hold back the tears, but they kept coming. "I was scared because you went away. You made me sleep in a mean way, and then you went away. It was already scary, then you did something mean. You were never mean. Never ever mean until then. Then you were gone, Mommy was sick, Daddy was sad about you and Mommy, and every-thing was wrong."

I looked at my uncle, my favorite creature in the whole world. "Everything is wrong, and nothing is ever going to be right again. And it's because of you. I love you, Uncle Mark, but I hate you too."

I stood, walked over to the chairs, and sat. But sitting wasn't good enough. This chair was puffy and soft. So I lay down, I curled into a ball, with my tail over my muzzle so nobody could see how hard I was crying.

———

"You have a 2D call from UC Penal. This call will be monitored. There is a 1.25-second lag on this call. Do you accept the conditions of this call?"

Louis looked at the message and hit the accept button.

Pat's face appeared on his tablet's screen. He looked tired, maybe a bit sick.

"Pat, are you all right?"

"Louis, I love you. I know… There you. I'll stop. Damn, I hate time lag. I'm fine."

Louis waited a moment to make sure Pat was done. "I love you, too. You don't look good, but it is so good to see you."

"I just got out of the spin and puke—the centrifugal gravity correction chamber—for two whole hours. I threw up three times, and I have to do kitchen duty when my time for this call is done. They actually synthesize the food raw and cook it up here. I'll have to brown raw, synthetic ground beef with synthetic onions or something like that. And if I throw up in the food, that will be so many demerits I'll be running up a mountain tomorrow or something."

Louis let Pat run out. He'd learned even without a second of communication lag that his husband sometimes needed to just talk.

"Take deep breaths. In through your nose, out through your mouth. It's probably what your therapist has been recommending for stress, but it works for nausea, at least from the spin and puke to."

He held up a paw to let Pat know he wasn't done. "I was stationed on Mars for a month between the Hawk and the Sparrow. I've spent my time in the Spin and Puke. Everything else they are making you do up there might be at least in part for punishment, but that is part of how the fleet keeps their members healthy and in shape to work in Earth, or slightly higher, gravity."

"I wasn't the only one who got sick. Even creatures who have been here… A bear named Callen, who has been here for five years, threw up. You don't know what it is like to smell bear puke from half a meter."

"Callen Mills… I've heard of him. Brilliant scientist. Was working on the fleet's faster-than-light program. But supposedly, he snapped over something and… I'd have to pull up the old news reports, but it was bad."

"Said he shredded half his bridge crew."

"That's right. Bear claws can be nasty. Multiple deaths, others medically discharged."

Louis leaned closer to the tablet. "Other than the spin and puke, how are you doing, really?"

"Louis, I don't know if I can make three years. Every day is the same mind-numbing, body-breaking thing. I thought watching the fuel flows was bad. But spending two hours a day walking, or walking just shy of running, staring at a blank wall, then lifting, calisthenics, dishes, cooking, lather, rinse, repeat…"

"What?"

"It comes from Pre-cataclysm shampoo bottles, they would put that on them as instructions to get people to use more so they could sell more, produce more plastic waste, use more petroleum, whatever stupid motives my Pre-cataclysm ancestors had for fu… ruining the world."

"You get demerits for using non-fleet language?"

"I get demerits for looking the wrong way. This system is designed to punish. When they say it is a punitive brig, they mean it."

"Patrick Bass, you have two years and fifty-one weeks before you get transferred to the rehabilitative brig. When that time comes, your husband, the wolf who loves you and you love, will be waiting for you. We'll be able to hold hands, paws, put your hand in my paw, however we can describe it. Maybe we'll even be able to…"

After a few seconds, he saw Pat smile at the suggestion.

"Louis, I love you. You are my light at the end of this tunnel. That and the memory that I deserve this at some level. I nearly let too many good fleeters get killed because I let myself believe my father's hate for far too long, to the point that I was ready to die because I thought loving you made me wrong."

"Pat, I love you, too. We'll get through this. Together apart."

CHAPTER 7

CHAPTER 7

Special Agent Joshua Bender sat in the witness chair facing the UC Parliament Select Committee on Terrorism. He reviewed his notes on his tablet, scanned the MPs sitting in two arcs facing him, then at Dorothy Travis, the calico cat lawyer from UCIS legal, sitting next to him.

The MPs crossed the regional and species constituencies that made up the UC Parliament, and were from both the coalition in power, a conservative block, and the opposition.

Member Liv Haley, a giant otter representing part of South America, the committee chair, looked at him. "Special Agent Bender, can you say that the threat from Humans First and European Great Ape Liberation has ended?"

"Member Haley, no, I cannot. The joint task force I headed has neutralized the active threats related to the plans put in place by the late Xandra Mathias."

He looked the otter in the eyes, wanting to drive home this point. "We believe that we have substantially dismantled much of Humans First, since it was led, financed, and effectively controlled by Xandra

Mathais. Her death might have denied us some potential intelligence, but she was unlikely to cooperate any more after her conviction than she had before."

He leaned back. "Others from her organization have proven more forthcoming, usually in exchange for reduced sentencing. We are investigating Human First's ties with other humanist organizations as well as their ties with violent non-human extremist groups."

Dylan McDowell, an opposition goat representing a goat constituency, leaned into his microphone. "Agent Bender, what kind of cooperation has your investigation received from the disgraced fleet ensign, Patrick Bass?"

"Ensign Bass' primary information was his ability to identify Xandra Mathias and help us identify the hidden equipment that had been placed into more than a dozen fleet ships, allowing her to communicate with officers on board."

"Have you identified other fleet officers working with Humans First or other humanist or extremist groups?" That came from Jedidiah Crawford, a mccaw in the majority representing tropical birds.

"That would be a question for Admiral Packard of Fleet Investigative Services. My task force was kept out of that part of the investigation."

An armadillo, Remi Trujillo, a minority representative from North America, leaned in. "Many of my constituents have been very concerned about the continuing activities of Reverend Franklin Bass. Reverend Bass has publicly condemned his son, even calling him a species traitor, and burning his birth certificate and pictures of him in his church as part of a sermon. I have a holo of that sermon from the church's own server."

The space between the witness table and the MPs was filled with the image of a Pre-cataclysm megachurch. Joshua had trouble seeing Patrick Bass in the fat human with grey hair standing behind the pulpit in a conservative shirt, but with an unbuttoned collar and no tie. "Some folks, even some humans, are calling Patrick Bass a hero for his actions both after his arrest and in court. But that creature that came from my late wife's womb is no hero."

The image of Franklin Bass then picked up an old paper Bible and opened it. "Whosoever lieth with a beast shall surely be put to death." He then flipped a few pages to another marked passage. "And if a man lie with a beast, he shall surely be put to death: and ye shall slay the beast." He then flipped back a few pages. "Thou shalt not lie with mankind, as with womankind: it is an abomination."

Bass then set the bible back on his pulpit and picked up two items. A projection over his head showed that one was a North American birth certificate listing Patrick Bass' birth, and the other was a hard copy of Patrick Bass' fleet commissioning photo. "While I cannot put that child whom my wife bore to death as the Bible demands, I will do so ceremonially. He then reached over and used the candles burning on the altar next to the pulpit and set both pieces of paper alight and held them until they nearly burned his fingers before dropping them on the ground."

"We are called as the people, not the creatures, the People of God to live by his word as given in inspired scripture. Human beings are those created in God's image. God's son came to save mankind. When the devil raised the lesser creatures to intelligence, that did not remove them from our dominion; that did not make them any less beasts."

Member Trujillo stopped the playback. He then looked at Bender. "What is your task force, and the UCIS as a whole, doing to keep creatures safe from this kind of extremism, this kind of radicalization?"

Erick Horton stood outside the burned-out house—the whole block stank of burnt wood, and that distinct odor that came when buildings burned.

"Two minutes until live," Erick's producer's voice came through the bud in his ear. "Satellite uplink confirmed."

Erick turned to his local aid. "How does the mane look?" A lot of folks at the network would tell him he was vain. But as the top lion reporter working the North American beat for Global News Network, his looks were as important as his journalistic skills. He knew that there were plenty of creatures of all species and genders who turned into his reports as much to look at him as for the stories he covered.

"Erick, it is fine. I touched it up before we went live half an hour ago."

"But the sun is now up."

"It's fine."

"One minute until live. Holo cameras and 2D camera feeds live. Erick, you look fine, now quit fidgeting with your tie."

He picked up his tablet and reviewed his notes, then looked across at the prompter to make sure that it had his script up and displayed. That was one of the tricks of live news that most creatures didn't know about. Live stand-up reports were as scripted as your favorite drama. You can't have your favorite reporter flubbing on the air.

"Anchor throwing to you in 5…4…3…2…1…"

"We now go live to Erick Horton in Abilene, North America, where a simple house fire has proven to be something more. Erick, what have we learned?"

"Thank you, Jessica. Last night at 2330, Abilene Fire and Rescue responded to an automated alarm for a house fire on Delano Street in Northern Abilene. When they arrived, they found a house fully engulfed in fire. Per standard fire procedures, they searched for living beings and then proceeded to put the fire out."

He then checked to make sure that the footage taken by the local crew, showing the 2D-only images of the fire being fought the previous night, was being aired.

"After the fire was under control, firefighters made a disturbing find."

In his earpiece, he heard the audio from the earlier 3D recording. "At approximately 0230, during the search of the structure, two bodies were found. One is a human and the other is feline. Both were found hanging by their necks from eyebolts placed into one of the second-floor ceiling beams. The Medical Examiner has preliminarily identified them as Lawson and Emely Henson, the homeowners. Lawson was a human, aged 32, and his wife Emely was a mountain lion."

Erick took over the live narration. "Abilene has become a hotbed of humanist activity, and especially activity targeting human/non-human couples in the weeks since Reverend Franklin Bass' fiery sermon, where he condemned his son's relationship with an unidentified non-human member or former member of the UC fleet."

He then leaned towards the 2D camera. "When GNN contacted Abilene First Baptist for comment, neither the church nor Reverend Bass had any comment."

The footage from the early morning press conference resumed, this time, with the UCIS agent in charge covering this part of North America. "We are coordinating with local authorities to gather all evidence. The UCIS is considering this a hate crime and is providing all of our resources as part of the investigation."

Erick then looked at the camera. "Jessica, Ameer, I will update you in half an hour if I learn anything new. Now back to you in New Brussels."

He waited until the tally lights went out to let his breath out.

———

We always celebrated New Year's at ship's time, not at the time of our Earthside house. Daddy kept the ship on what they called UTC, or Common Earth Time. He said some folks still called it "Zulu," which was a really, really old name for it, way Pre-cataclysm.

The sun had set a couple of hours earlier, and it was dark outside. The snow was falling heavily. Benji had looked out the back porch and said it was already almost half a meter. That was too deep. I wasn't 750 millimeters tall yet, so half a meter of snow would be so much that I couldn't walk through it.

But Daddy had built a real fire in the old fireplace that came with our house. Our house was new, only built just before Mommy and Daddy moved in, shortly before Benji was born, a little more than thirteen years ago. But the fireplace was here from the Pre-cataclysm house that had stood here, and the house had been built to use it. It was big. I could stand in the fireplace without touching my ears to the top. It used a lot of stuff to synthesize enough wood for a fire, and when it burned, it polluted the air instead of going back into the—this is gross—toilet to be reused by the synthesizers. So Mommy and

Daddy only made fires on really special occasions, like New Year's Eve if it was really snowing hard outside.

Mommy had made a special roast, from real meat, not synthesized. And baked fresh bread using real flour and honey, and her sourdough mother. And we all had cups of eggnog, which had come from the synthesizer.

I'd been sneaking cups of eggnog from the synthesizer since the program had become available, at least until Mommy caught me and locked it so it would only make it for her and Daddy. I think it was because I once accidentally pushed the button and made the kind that tasted really funny and not good, and made my head spinny.

We were sitting at the table with most of the roast gone. Benji, who seemed to be eating more than Daddy all of a sudden, was using the last of the loaf of bread to soak up tiny bits of juice from the roast.

Daddy looked at his watch. "It's almost time." He then started counting. "10…9…8…7…"

We all joined in. "6…5…4…3…2…1…Happy New Year."

Mommy picked up her glass, which had something adult in it, instead of water like Benji, Krissy, and me. "Here's to 367 being a better year than 366."

Daddy picked up his glass and tapped it to Mommy's. "Here, here!"

I thought about how bad last year had been. It had good bits. I'd been to Mars three times and met a human. But then Uncle Mark…

"Mommy, Daddy, can I call Uncle Mark?"

Mommy looked at Daddy, who nodded.

"Let's all give Mark a New Year's call."

He walked over and picked up his tablet.

I looked at them. "Daddy, I need to talk to Uncle Mark before anyone else. Please."

"OK, Kitto. But I need to talk to the folks at the Rehab facility before they can put him on, all right?"

"OK."

I waited as Daddy made the call and talked to a few folks. He then handed me the tablet.

It had the "Please Stand By" screen up. Then Uncle Mark came on.

He was wearing his bright yellow jumpsuit and had his multi-colored arm on. He was in a tiny room, smaller than my bedroom, which is bigger than I need. But he's a grown-up and used to an entire house when Earthside.

"Uncle Mark. I don't hate you. I love you. I'm sorry I said I hate you."

"I know Danno. You were scared. I am sorry I hurt you. But when I shot you, and when I did everything else. I did it because I thought you were in danger, you understand that, don't you?"

"I know. I love you more 'cus of that."

"Is that the only reason you called?"

"Yes, but everyone else wants to talk to you, too."

"OK."

I handed the tablet to Daddy, who led everyone into the living room, where we sat with our backs to the fire. Once we were all sitting by the fire, we all looked at the tablet. "Happy New Year's, Uncle Mark."

ABOUT THE AUTHOR

Randall Fox is the pseudonym Ron Oakes uses when writing novellas about Randall and his friends.

Ron Oakes is a computer scientist, science fiction and fantasy fan, and self-published fantasy writer based in Albuquerque, New Mexico. Some of his earliest memories include watching *Star Trek* on weekday afternoons and desiring to work on computers like those found on the U.S.S. Enterprise. Not long afterward, he saw *Star Wars* in its original incarnation (before it became *Episode IV: A New Hope*).

In the late 1970s, through his Boy Scouts troop, he was introduced to Dungeons & Dragons. At around the same time, he was introduced to the *Chronicles of Prydain* by Lloyd Alexander. These combined to create a love of fantasy.

After college, he moved to the Chicago Suburbs. His love of D&D and other tabletop role-playing games led him to discover organized Science Fiction Fandom in the early 1990s. As a fan and convention runner, he has worked on and run conventions in Chicago, San Diego, and Albuquerque.

He is married to another fan and works as a government contractor in Albuquerque. He shares his house with his wife, four cats, over 300 robots, multiple lightsabers, more artwork than the walls can hold, several dragons, and assorted stuffed animals—not all of which are from this world.

ALSO BY RANDALL FOX

UNITED CREATURES UNIVERE STORIES

Freight, Family and Fire

Half-Tonne of Silence

RANDALL FOX STORIES

Flight of the Heretics

The Prey's Rebellion

The Wolf and The Parliament

The Hermitage and The Henge

The Tunnel and The Ox

The Duchess and The Fox

The Cougar and The Quest

The Books and The Guardian

The Kitsune and The Kit

The Transformation and The Future

The Pup and The Adventure

The Moose and The Crown

The Stoat and The Pilgrims

The Muzzle and The Pursuit

The Potion and The Madness

The Priest and The Gang

The Lord and The Fires

The Wolf and The Champion

The Bear and The Squirrel

The Reindeer and the Stone Circle

The Catacombs and The Wolf

The Friends and The Walk

The Trickster and The Cabin

The Fox and The Letter

The Mouse and The Squirrels

The Executor and The Revenge

INSPECTOR BEAUREGARD STORIES

The Inspector and The Robber

The Inspector and The Magistrate

The Inspector And His Son

The Advocate and The Duke

———

AS RON OAKES

The Phoenix Knives